D1295636

# MABEL takes a SAIL

# MABEL takes a SAIL

*By* Emily Chetkowski

*Illustrated by* Dawn Peterson

J.N. TOWNSEND PUBLISHING
EXETER, NEW HAMPSHIRE
2000

Printed in Canada.

Published by

J. N. Townsend Publishing
12 Greenleaf Drive
Exeter, New Hampshire 03833
800/333-9883
www.jntownsendpublishing.com


ISBN: 1-880158-26-4

Library of Congress Cataloging-in-Publication Data

Chetkowski, Emily.
    Mabel takes a sail / by Emily Chetkowski; illustrated by Dawn Peterson.
        p. cm.
    Summary: Mabel the dog goes sailing off the coast of Maine with her family and is kept busy by their new pet, an inexperienced dog named Maxine.

    1. Dogs--Juvenile fiction. [1. Dogs--Fiction. 2. Sailing--Fiction. 3. Maine--Fiction.] I. Peterson, Dawn, ill. II. title

PZ10.3.C4165 Mad 2000
[E]--dc21                                                                    00-037426

10 9 8 7 6 5 4 3 2

To Mabel, forever.

# Acknowledgments

A special thank you to:

The United States Coast Guard for their advice on boating safety; Dave Grisaru of Islesboro's Big Tree Boating Community Sailing Program for helping me fine tune my nautical skills; Ralph Gray for taking me around Islesboro on his boat *The Growler*, while I researched this story; Jeremy Townsend, a breath of fresh air in the publishing world, whose professionalism, insight and integrity continue to amaze me; and to Christine Coombs for being a friend.

ELC

It was another breezy day on the island of Islesboro. There wasn't a cloud in the sky, and the sunlight made Penobscot Bay sparkle like glass. It was a perfect day for a sail, and Mabel was ready to go. She was excited as she watched her family put her life jacket in the car. They really *were* taking her sailing today! But then she saw them packing gear for another dog. Oh no—they were taking Maxine as well!

"This ought to be interesting," thought Mabel grumpily.

Maxine had never been on a boat other than the island ferry. She didn't know the first thing about going sailing. In fact, she didn't know that they were going anywhere right now. She was too busy chasing a red squirrel. This was nothing unusual. Maxine was just an overgrown puppy. She thought it was her job to keep all uninvited critters out of the yard. No one was safe. Rosie the cat and the chickens, Stanley, Wanda and Zelda were often targets, too.

Maxine collected treasures. Unfortunately they were usually things that belonged to someone else. She'd leap high in the air to take laundry off the clothesline or grab a hat off a kid's head. She even brought home a lobsterman's buoys and someone's dirty old socks. Her family returned the buoys right away, but no one admitted to owning the smelly socks.

Now it was time to leave and Maxine was nowhere in sight. Everyone was looking for her. Mabel realized they were never going to get to the boat if she didn't help them out. Just like Maxine, Mabel had a job too, only it wasn't chasing squirrels—it was chasing Maxine!

"Oh, what a bother," grumbled Mabel as she trotted off to join in the search.

Poor Mabel. She had adjusted well to having two children in the family. In fact, she really adored the kids, but having Maxine around was just too much. Sometimes Mabel tried to teach her the difference between right and wrong, and how to be a good dog. It was quite a chore.

That youngster had a lot to learn.

Maxine was truly a pest. She loved to pull on Mabel's ears and whack her in the head with her big white paw. Ambushing Mabel was another favorite pastime. With no warning, Maxine would run and crash into Mabel at full speed, and that is exactly what she did today when Mabel found her. Maxine thought it was funny. Mabel thought it was annoying, not to mention painful.

"Ouch," whimpered Mabel. She thought briefly about pouncing back, but she was more interested in doing something else—going sailing!

Getting Maxine into the car took forever. Mabel got pounced on a few more times in the process. The dogs sat in the back with the kids as they set off for the boat.On the way, Mabel stuck her head out the window to smell the sea breeze and look at the beckoning bay. Maxine, on the other hand, didn't even notice they were near an ocean. She was too busy trying to lick everyone. Even the adults in the front didn't escape Maxine's slobber.

The boat, *Off Call*, was out on its mooring. Mabel knew they would use the dinghy to get to it. Being a skilled seafaring dog, she also knew just what to do when using a small rowboat. For instance, it's important to keep the dinghy balanced at all times to avoid tipping it. So Mabel stayed low and carefully stepped into the center of the boat, then sat right down. Of course, she already had her life jacket on. Mabel was a great swimmer, but she knew how quickly accidents can happen, and how cold the Maine waters can be. Wearing a life jacket was the smart thing to do.

Maxine had a long way to go before she could ever be called seafaring. While Mabel was boarding the dinghy, Maxine slipped her collar. She charged down the dock and jumped head-first into the boat, crashing into Mabel!

Splash! The dinghy tipped and both dogs fell overboard. Maxine wasn't wearing her life jacket. She sank under the cool water, but soon surfaced, struggling to swim. Floating nicely, Mabel dog-paddled over to Maxine, grabbed her by the ear and pulled her toward the dock, where they were both lifted safely out of the water.

"Yikes!" thought Mabel as she shook herself off. "This trip is certainly not off to a good start."

Once the dinghy was properly loaded, dogs and all, the row out to the boat was easy. Soon they were off the mooring and underway, motoring down Gilkey's Harbor.

"What's our port-of-call today?" Mabel wondered as they made their way through narrow Brackett's Channel. Her guess was Pulpit's Harbor, dead ahead on North Haven Island. It was a short sail and a favorite spot to anchor for lunch.

As they left the channel and entered East Penobscot Bay, Mabel's family pointed the boat into the wind to hoist the main and jib sails. The southwest breeze filled the sails nicely as they turned the boat to run north up the bay. Now their destination was obvious.

"We're sailing all the way around Islesboro!" thought Mabel as she barked and pranced about with delight.

Most of the trip would be an easy run up the bay. However, once they passed the northernmost point of the island, they'd turn south directly into the wind. Mabel knew that a sailboat can't sail directly into the wind. They'd have to tack and turn back and forth, beating down West Penobscot Bay to make it home. That could be a nuisance.

Speaking of nuisances, Maxine was actually behaving for a change. She had her life jacket on and was sitting still, enjoying the sail.

"This is a first," thought Mabel.

But Mabel was also thinking about something else. The wind was picking up and the boat was moving right along. Sailing is fun but it can be dangerous, especially if you don't know what you're doing. Mabel decided it was time to show Maxine the ropes, and she would do so by setting a good example.

Mabel knew the sails could jibe without warning. The mainsail's boom could quickly swing from one side of the boat to another. So she kept her head low and paid attention.

"Ready to jibe?" called out Dad, the helmsman. When the helmsman sailing the boat calls out an order, everyone needs to listen!

"Ready," replied the crew and everyone else on board.

"Woof," barked Mabel to let them know she was ready. Maxine looked ready, too.

"Jibe ho," said the helmsman, hauling the mainsheet to ease the sail over from port to starboard.

Just as the wind filled the mainsail and pushed it over hard, Maxine ran up on deck to bark at a seal that had popped up near the boat.

Whack! The boom hit Maxine. She fell backwards into the water for another chilly little swim.

"Man overboard," shouted the kids. Mabel thought, "Pest overboard."

Quickly, they turned the boat around while hauling in the sails. They pointed the boat dead into the wind to stop it alongside the soggy dog. Mabel's family hoisted her aboard, using the boat hook to grab her by the life jacket. Unhurt, Maxine said thank you by shaking off all over everyone and giving them big salty dog licks. Mabel went below decks to get as far away from her as possible.

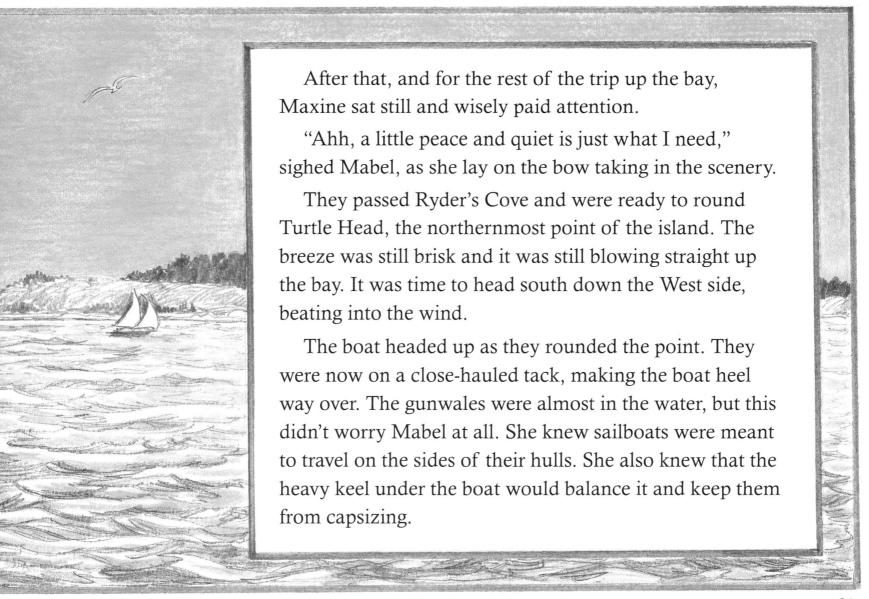

After that, and for the rest of the trip up the bay, Maxine sat still and wisely paid attention.

"Ahh, a little peace and quiet is just what I need," sighed Mabel, as she lay on the bow taking in the scenery.

They passed Ryder's Cove and were ready to round Turtle Head, the northernmost point of the island. The breeze was still brisk and it was still blowing straight up the bay. It was time to head south down the West side, beating into the wind.

The boat headed up as they rounded the point. They were now on a close-hauled tack, making the boat heel way over. The gunwales were almost in the water, but this didn't worry Mabel at all. She knew sailboats were meant to travel on the sides of their hulls. She also knew that the heavy keel under the boat would balance it and keep them from capsizing.

"Ready about?" the helmsman cried out. It was Mom this time, and she needed to tack.

"Ready," replied the crew.

"Woof," barked Mabel.

"Yip," barked Maxine as she dove to the floor of the cockpit and tried to hide in the corner.

"Hard Alee!" the helmsman said as she pushed the tiller and turned the boat through the wind, changing tack. The boat immediately heeled over on its other side.

Poor Maxine was scared out of her wits. She had already been in the cold water enough today and had no desire to go swimming again!

Mabel went over and leaned against Maxine to comfort her, and to keep her out of the way of more trouble.

Soon, everyone on board was enjoying the sail as the boat charged past Marshall's Cove, and headed toward Grindle Point. As they neared Gooseberry Nubble, the island ferry was just setting off for the mainland. The *Off Call* tacked to avoid getting in its way.

Watching the ferry leave Islesboro, Mabel thought about the trip off the island she took on it once, all by herself and without permission. She especially remembered the tasty treats she got at the waterfront lobster restaurant that day while waiting for her family to rescue her and sail her back to the island.

"I really must go there again sometime," she decided, sniffing the air to smell the food cooking.

Once the ferry passed, they trimmed the sails to stay on their heading. The kids knew what was coming next. Excited, they went up on the foredeck. Mabel knew what was coming, too, but stayed right where she was, keeping Maxine with her. She didn't like the ferry's wake and the way it made the boat bob up and down.

Splash! The sailboat slammed into the wake's big waves, riding them like a roller coaster and spraying water all over the kids. They were soaked but they loved it.

Soon, it was time to head into home port and call it a day. After one more tack to pass the lighthouse and round the point, they picked up their mooring, and dropped the sails. Once the boat was secure and shipshape, the kids hauled in the dinghy to load it up.

Mabel hated to go ashore, but it was time. Besides she had people to meet and places to go, as always. So when she was told to, Mabel carefully stepped into the dinghy and sat right down. Just as she did, she happened to look up.

"Oh no, not again!" thought Mabel. There was Maxine, hanging over the side of the boat, about to fall right smack on top of her!

That was all that Mabel had to see.

"Land Ho!" barked quick-thinking Mabel. She jumped into the water and dog-paddled herself back to shore. She had had enough of Maxine's antics for one day.

Mabel shook off while she watched her family row in. Amazingly, Maxine had stayed safely seated in the bow of the dinghy. Mabel was proud of her, but she was also pretty pleased with herself. She had taught Maxine well.

"I'm such a good dog," she thought, wagging her tail. "And I surely deserve a treat," she decided as she trotted off towards the ferry, hoping for a ride and another lobster dinner.

THE END

# Glossary of Nautical Terms

**beat:** to sail toward the direction the wind is coming from, by making tack after tack

**boom:** the part of the boat the mainsail is attached to that holds it out from the mast. It can swing from side to side across the cockpit.

**bow:** the front end of a boat

**buoys:** an anchored float. Small, colorful ones are tied onto lobster traps so lobstermen can find their traps.

**capsize:** when a boat tips over in the water

**change tack:** to change the direction a sailboat is going by turning the bow across the wind

**channel:** narrow waterway that boats follow to get from one body of water to another

**close-hauled:** sailing as close as possible toward the wind

**cockpit:** outside seating area on a boat

**deck:** the topside of the boat that you can walk on

**dinghy:** small sail or row boat, usually used to get to a larger boat at anchor

**dock:** platform that a boat is pulled up to in order to board it

**ferry:** boat used to carry people across water. Usually used to get to an island.

**foredeck:** the part of the deck in the front of the boat

**gunwale:** upper edge of the side of a boat, where the side meets the deck

**hauling the mainsheet:** pulling on the rope used to adjust the main sail

**hard alee:** pushing the tiller away from the wind to change direction

**heeling:** when the force of the wind on the sails causes the sailboat to lean over and sail more on its side

**helmsman:** person who steers the boat

**hoist the main:** raise the mainsail

**homeport:** a boat's home, where it is usually kept

**hull:** the bottom of the boat

**jib sail:** the smaller sail found in the front of the sailboat

**jibe:** to change direction when the wind is coming from behind the boat

**jibe ho:** what the helmsman says to warn passengers that they are about to jibe

**keel:** the weighted bottom of a sailboat that helps keep it upright

**Land Ho:** land in sight

**life jacket:** a vest worn to keep a person floating in water. Dogs have special life jackets to fit a four-legged body

**mooring:** a heavy permanent anchor that a boat is tied up to while in the water

**port of call:** where a boat is traveling to

**port side:** the left side of a boat

**run:** to sail with the wind coming from behind the boat

**seafaring:** travels the seas

**shipshape:** neat and tidy

**starboard:** the right side of the boat

**tack:** change direction on a sailboat to take advantage of the wind

**tiller:** a long handle attached to a boat's rudder, used to steer the boat

**trim the sails:** adjust the sails to take advantage of the wind

**wake:** waves made by a boat moving through the water

# OFF CALL

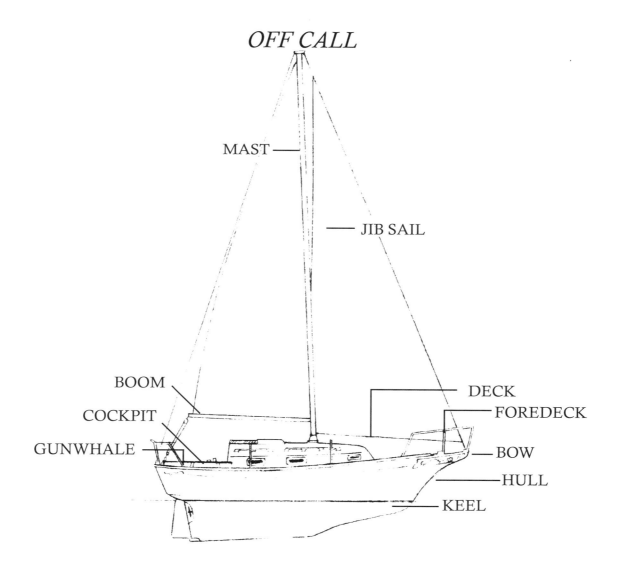

MAST

JIB SAIL

BOOM

COCKPIT

DECK

FOREDECK

GUNWHALE

BOW

HULL

KEEL

## About the Author

Emily Chetkowski is the author of Mabel Takes the Ferry, and *Amasa Walker's Splendid Garment*. She shares her home in Massachusetts with her family and assorted animals, including two horses, Sheila and Shenanigans. Emily summers in Islesboro, Maine, where she does most of her writing, when she's not out sailing with the dogs.

## About the Illustrator

Dawn Peterson is a free-lance illustrator living on the Maine coast, where she has two daughters, four grandchildren and two cats. She especially enjoys drawing animals. This is the sixth children's book that she has illustrated, including *Mabel Takes the Ferry* and the L.L. Bear series for Down East Books.

## About Mabel

Since the success of her first book, Mabel has been busy traveling New England to meet her many fans. Fame hasn't spoiled her, though, as she still enjoys the simple pleasures in life, such as swimming in the ocean, eating the cat's food, and barking at absolutely nothing, along with cleverly managing to hide from Maxine whenever possible.

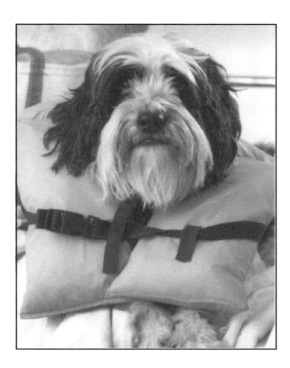

## and Maxine

True to her Border Collie roots, Maxine enjoys herding the cats and chickens, and keeping the goat out of the garden when she isn't busy splashing around in the fish pond, or tagging along with the horses on a trail ride.